# It's Summertime!

by Elaine W. Good
Illustrated by Susie Shenk Wenger

Good Books
Intercourse, PA 17534

It's Summertime!
Copyright © 1989, 1995 by Good Books, Intercourse, PA 17534
First published in 1991.
New Paperback edition published in 1995.
International Standard Book Number: 1-56148-144-0
Library of Congress Catalog Card Number: 89-28895
Printed in Canada

**Library of Congress Cataloging-in-Publication Data**
Good, Elaine W., 1944-
   It's summertime!/by Elaine W. Good; illustrated by Susie Shenk Wenger.
      p. cm.
   Summary: For a child living on a farm, the joys of summer include strawberries, playful cows, haymaking, and sweet corn.
   [1. Summer—Fiction. 2. Farm life—Fiction.] I. Wenger, Susie Shenk, 1956-   ill.
II. Title.
PZ7.G5996It  1989
[E[—dc 20                                        89-28895

It's summer! I know it is! Want to know how I know?
Strawberries! I went to inspect the patch and red was peeking out
from the bright green leaves. Uh-oh! They are still white underneath.
But I can't wait. They taste good anyhow.

There's no time like summertime!

Today we let the cows go into the meadow. After being in the barn since late fall, they gallop, jump, and butt into each other, kicking as if there were springs in their feet!

There's no time like summertime!

Oh it is hot! I take off my shoes and run barefooted across the soft, cool grass. When I get to the driveway, I have to walk on my tippee toes. Ouch! The stones hurt. I guess shoes feel good after all. Mommy says I'll get used to it.

There's no time like summertime!

The weatherman says it won't rain today. Good. That means we can make hay! I watch Mommy drive the tractor while Daddy stacks the bales on a wagon behind the baler. Then we take the wagons to the big barn where I help unload them. Those bales are heavy! There's no time like summertime!

One warm evening after a long day of picking peas, Mommy sits on the bridge. She watches while I make my boat swooosh through the water. Big splashes are the best!

There's no time like summertime!

I must help Christine feed the little heifers. Lilac almost bumps me over, trying to get her nose into the bucket of milk. I watch her tail wagging like she has a motor inside. I scratch her head as she slurps the last of her milk and tries to lick my nose!

There's no time like summertime!

Today our family took the day off and went to the zoo. We had lots of fun feeding elephants and watching cockatoos swoop around their big room.

There's no time like summertime!

The grass in the lawn is so tall it almost hides my tractor. After
Caroline is finished mowing, I get my toys and pretend to bale hay.
There's no time like summertime!

On hot, sticky afternoons Christine and I cool off by swimming in
the creek in our meadow. Sometimes big, nosy heifers come to watch
us. Christine makes a big splash and I shout to frighten them away.
There's no time like summertime!

Tonight the kitchen was so full of jars and spoons and canning kettles that we carried our supper outside and ate at the table in the yard. We roasted hot dogs, and when the meal was finished we used the last coals in the fire to make gooey toasted marshmallows.

There's no time like summertime!

Boom! Flash! Rain is coming. Mommy and I cover the sandbox. Daddy and David run to close the barn doors. Christine and Caroline gather our toys and lawn chairs. Then we all hurry into the house to close windows and wait for the storm to pass. When the air is calm again, the lawn is littered with sticks.

There's no time like summertime!

After chores tonight we mix up eggs, cream, and sugar for homemade ice cream. We take turns cranking until we are tired and the ice cream is hard. Then we have a double treat. Just as we sit down to eat our tasty snack, a red fox streaks across the meadow and disappears into the cornfield.

There's no time like summertime!

We have sweet corn in the garden. Lots of it. I could eat it every dinner and supper! Daddy and Mommy say we have enough to share with Effie Snyder who doesn't keep a garden anymore. Caroline harnesses Rusty to the cart, and we head for Effie's with a grocery bag stuffed with corn.

There's no time like summertime!

corn for Effie

It's time for Family Gathering! Grandpa,
Grandma, my uncles, aunts, and cousins are all
coming to our farm for three days! We sleep out in
tents, play hide 'n seek, take swing rides, play
baseball in the meadow, and sing songs together.

There's no time like summertime!

Geese! I hear their honking and jump out of bed. From the window I see a whole flock land in the creek and the meadow. Shi-i-i-sh-sh-sh goes the water when they splash down. There are a hundred of them! David says when fall comes the geese will fly south. Fall. So that's what happens when summer is over.

Elaine W. Good lives on a farm near Lititz, Pa. She and her husband are parents to two sons and two daughters.

Susie Shenk Wenger is an illustrator who lives in State College, Pa., with her husband and young daughter.

*That's What Happens When It's Spring! Fall Is Here! I Love It!* and *White Wonderful Winter!* are the other books in this seasonal series by Good and Shenk Wenger.